BOULDER CITY LIBRARY

3 1432 00084 6046

D0603940

E   Ada, Alma Flor

Malachite palace

Boulder City Library
701 Adams Blvd.
Boulder City, NV 89005

DISCARD

THE
MALACHITE
PALACE

by Alma Flor Ada

translated by Rosa Zubizarreta

illustrated by Leonid Gore

BOULDER CITY LIBRARY

BOULDER CITY, NV 89005-2697

DISCARD

ATHENEUM BOOKS FOR YOUNG READERS

AUG 1999

To Cristina Isabel, welcome to the planet, and in loving memory
of Willis Gortner II, architect of beautiful buildings, friendships,
and his two greatest works, Chris and Eric

—A. F. A.

To Emily, my little princess who will have a lot of friends

—L. G.

Atheneum Books for Young Readers
An imprint of Simon & Schuster Children's Publishing Division
1230 Avenue of the Americas
New York, New York 10020
Text copyright © 1998 by Alma Flor Ada
Illustrations copyright © 1998 by Leonid Gore
All rights reserved including the right of reproduction in whole or in part in any form.
Book design by Angela Carlino
The text of this book is set in Kabel.
The illustrations are rendered in acrylic paint and ink.
First Edition
Printed in Hong Kong by South China Printing Co. (1988) Ltd.
10 9 8 7 6 5 4 3 2 1
Library of Congress Cataloging-in-Publication Data
Ada, Alma Flor.
The malachite palace / by Alma Flor Ada ; translated by Rosa Zubizarreta ;
illustrated by Leonid Gore.—1st ed.
p.   cm.
Summary: A tiny yellow bird helps a lonely princess learn the truth about songs,
freedom, and the children who are playing beyond the palace gates.
ISBN 0-689-31972-X
[1. Fairy tales—Fiction. 2. Princesses—Fiction.
3. Birds—Fiction. 4. Prejudices—Fiction.]
I. Zubizarreta-Ada, Rosalma. II. Gore, Leonid, ill. III. Title.
PZ8.A2137Mal   1998
[E]—dc20
95-44676

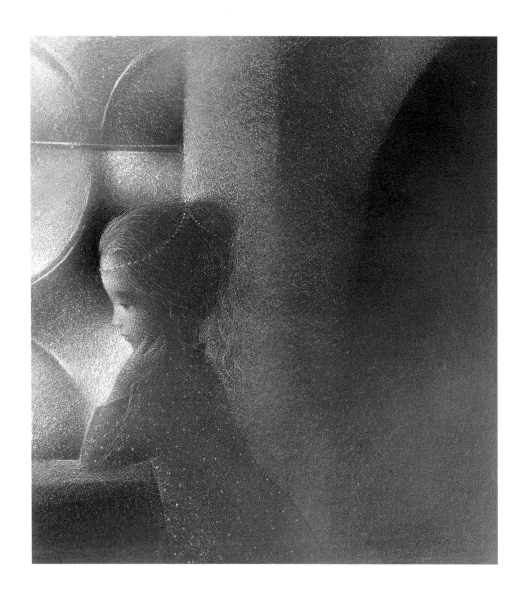

There once was a princess who lived in a malachite palace. She had everything she could possibly want. Everything, that is, except for a friend.

On the other side of ornate iron gates, many children laughed and played in the fields beyond the palace. But neither the lady-in-waiting, all dressed in white, nor the governess, all dressed in black—and much less the queen, all dressed in gold—would have thought, even for a moment, that the princess could be allowed to play with the other children.

"Those children are rude!"

"Those children are ignorant!"

"Those children are common!" they would say, as if in a chorus.

And so the princess always kept the windows of her room in the malachite palace tightly closed so that the voices of the children playing in the open fields would not reach her. Perhaps she had come to believe what her elders said about those children; or perhaps she just didn't want to be reminded of how happy the children sounded as they scampered about.

One windy morning in early spring, the princess heard a *tap, tap, tap* at her window. She looked and saw a cherry branch, heavy with blossoms. When she opened the window to reach the flowers, a little bird flew into the room.

It was a tiny yellow bird, with bright black eyes. And when he opened his beak to sing, a light and joyful music filled the palace.

"Quickly, quickly!" cried the princess as she closed the window. "Come catch him, come catch him!"

The lady-in-waiting appeared immediately with a towel in hand, while the governess hastily took off her black shawl. Between the two of them, they soon captured the tiny bird and locked him in a silver cage.

"What a rare and precious bird!" said the queen. "It's very fitting that he chose to come to my princess."

"How cultured," said the governess.

"How elegant," said the lady-in-waiting.

The princess wanted very much to hear the bird sing again. But many days went by, and the tiny bird did not let forth even a small warble.

"I'm sure that he knows how to sing," said the princess. "The day we caught him, he sang beautifully."

"Let's bring him chocolate," said the lady-in-waiting.

"Or caviar," suggested the governess.

"Let's gild his silver cage," ordered the queen. "He will certainly sing for us once he has a golden cage."

But in spite of all their efforts, the little bird remained silent.

Maybe he needs some air, thought the princess. *Perhaps he misses the fragrance of the flowers. . . .* So she opened the window and placed the birdcage on her balcony. When she did this, the bird began to sing once more. But his song was sad and feeble, unlike the joyful song he had brought with him when he first arrived.

Since the window was now kept open, the little princess could once again hear the sounds of the children playing in the fields. And she noticed that each time the children laughed, the bird would perk up a little, and his song became brighter. Sometimes when the bird sang, the children would peek into the palace gardens through the iron fence.

"How unseemly!" said the lady-in-waiting.

"How ill-mannered!" complained the governess.

"I'll put a stop to it!" announced the queen. And she ordered vines planted inside the iron fence. Soon the vines grew thick and tall, and the children's faces could no longer be seen, nor their laughter heard, from inside the palace.

When summer came, the vines grew even thicker. In the fall, the leaves changed color, and the palace seemed to be surrounded by walls of fire. Meanwhile, the tiny bird's song was becoming sadder and quieter every day. Finally, it stopped altogether.

The princess tried everything she could think of to cheer him up. She told the bird the story of how his beautiful cage, a gift from a faraway emperor, had arrived at the palace balanced atop a tower of presents all carried by a white elephant. She hummed her favorite lullaby, and offered him dry dates and figs. But the bird remained silent.

As the days grew colder, the princess moved the cage with the silent bird indoors. One morning, after all the leaves from the vines had fallen, the princess opened the door to the balcony. *Maybe if the bird sees the sky and fields again, he'll want to sing once more,* she thought. As she stood with the cage on the balcony, she heard the voices of the children playing outside the gates. They shouted and laughed as they slid over the snow with their sleds, and built a large snowman with a full, round face.

The princess listened to the children's voices, longing to join them. Then without knowing quite why, she opened the door to the cage and let the tiny yellow bird fly away.

For many days, the princess looked and looked at the empty cage, and listened to the sounds of the children as they played in the snow.

One morning, she woke up and saw frost covering the window. The princess called out for a lackey: "Quickly, quickly, I need some tools!"

And then the little princess, who had never before held a needle, a thimble, nor even a pair of scissors in her hands, began to work with the tools. Clumsily at first, and then more confidently, she managed to unhinge the delicate door of the cage. Next, she unfastened some of the bars from the other side. Now the cage resembled an open archway.

Then the princess said:

"Quickly, quickly, I want sunflower seeds, and millet, and nuts!"

And she filled the open cage with food, and placed it on the balcony.

That afternoon, as the setting sun turned the snow into a crimson blanket, the princess saw many hungry birds pecking at the seeds. In the midst of the bright red cardinals, the feisty blue jays, the brown-and-white chickadees, and the soft gray sparrows stood the tiny yellow bird.

"You've come back!" she cried. "And you've brought your friends."

The yellow bird took a sunflower seed in his beak and flew back over the iron fence.

The princess watched him fly away. The laughter of the children playing outside seemed more joyful than ever. She ran to the palace fence and opened the ornate gates.

And when the lady-in-waiting, in her starched white coif, the governess, in her black silk dress, and the queen, in her gold evening gown, said:

"You can't play with those children. They are rude!"

"And ignorant!"

"And common!"

The little princess answered:

"That's not true! That's not true! That's not true!"

Then she ran into the fields beyond the iron gates. There her laughter mingled with the laughter of the other children, while the yellow bird, perched on a leafless vine, sang louder and more sweetly than it ever had before.